CLARENCE'S BIG SECRET

By

Christine MacGregor Cation
& Roy MacGregor

Illustrated by

Mathilde Cinq-Mars

OWLKIDS BOOKS

This is the very real story of CLARENCE BRAZIER, who was born a long time ago, on a farm deep in the Canadian woods.

For nearly one hundred years, Clarence had a big secret.

Clarence was the third of seven children. The boys—all six of them—slept in one room, three to a bed.

On cold winter nights, Clarence always nabbed the warm spot in the middle. In the morning, he would let his brothers go to the outhouse first—that way the seat would be warm for his turn.

Clarence was always thinking!

Clarence was big for his age and strong. By the age of six, he was milking the cows, harnessing the workhorses, Boxer and Biddy, and carrying heavy bales of hay.

On his first day of school, Clarence eagerly took a seat in the front row with the other first graders.

"Welcome," said the teacher with a smile. Sure that Clarence belonged in grade three because of his size, she asked him to stand and spell his name.

Clarence didn't even know the alphabet yet. As he stood there, frozen, some of the students began to snigger. And that was that. Clarence burst from his seat and ran all the way home.

Clarence would never attend school again.
Soon after that first day, his father was
blinded in a terrible accident.

"I will take care of the farm,"
Clarence vowed.

And he did just that. By the time he was
seven, Clarence was doing his father's
chores as well as his own. The two made
extra money by cutting trees to sell
for firewood. Clarence would choose a
tree, he and his father would cut it, and
then Clarence would guide his father to
safety before the tree fell.

Barely into his teens, Clarence went to work as a logger. His winters were spent felling trees. In spring, he nimbly guided logs downriver to the mills.

The men in the bush camp loved having Clarence around. On long winter evenings, he taught the men how to square dance, clacking spoons to keep the beat and calling out the steps. Some of the men would even tuck tea towels into their belts, like skirts, so they could dance the ladies' parts.

The owner wanted to make Clarence boss of the bush camp. But Clarence was terrified the job would expose his big secret. So he quit.

Clarence headed north to work in the gold mines. One day, a young woman caught his eye and so distracted him, he ran his bike into the ditch.

"I thought that was a big snake," Clarence said, pointing to a twisted branch on the road, "so I pulled over to save you from it."

Clarence's ridiculous explanation made Angela laugh. They began courting and soon decided to marry.

Clarence didn't want to keep his secret from Angela, so just before their wedding day, he plucked up his courage. "I have something to tell you," he said. "But first, please promise that you will never tell anyone."

Angela promised. And for the first time ever, Clarence shared his secret.

Clarence did well at the mine, and soon the boss offered him a promotion. Even though it meant more money, Clarence feared his secret would get out, and he quit.

Clarence needed a job where his secret wouldn't get in the way. So he and Angela bought a farm and began to raise crops and animals—and a family. They had four daughters. They were good farmers and so successful, they even had an indoor toilet!

The girls adored their dad. He was kind. And funny. And a great practical joker. He gave them nicknames. Pearl was "Muskrat" because she was a hard worker. Doris became "Corky" because she had been a chunky baby. Janet was "Razorblade" because she was skinny and sharp. Irene, the baby, he called "Archie"—because Clarence had always wanted a boy!

None of his daughters knew their father's secret.

Years passed. The girls finished their schooling, married, and had families of their own.

Clarence was a wonderful grandfather! He told stories, sang songs, and played harmonica lullabies for the little ones. He gave piggyback rides. And when his grandchildren were old enough, he taught them how to cut firewood and prune raspberry bushes to produce the biggest, juiciest berries.

Shortly after her eightieth birthday, Angela passed away. She and Clarence had been married for sixty-five years.

Clarence was heartbroken. And worried. With Angela's help, he had hidden his big secret for ninety-three years. It was Angela who had made the lists and done the shopping, handled the mail and paid the bills, written the letters and signed the report cards.

All because Clarence did not know how to read.

Clarence needed to find a way to live on the farm
without Angela's help. So he came up with a plan.
He would teach himself to read.

His first schoolbooks were junk mail. He took sales
flyers and matched pictures—bicycles, lawn mowers,
frying pans—to the words beside them.

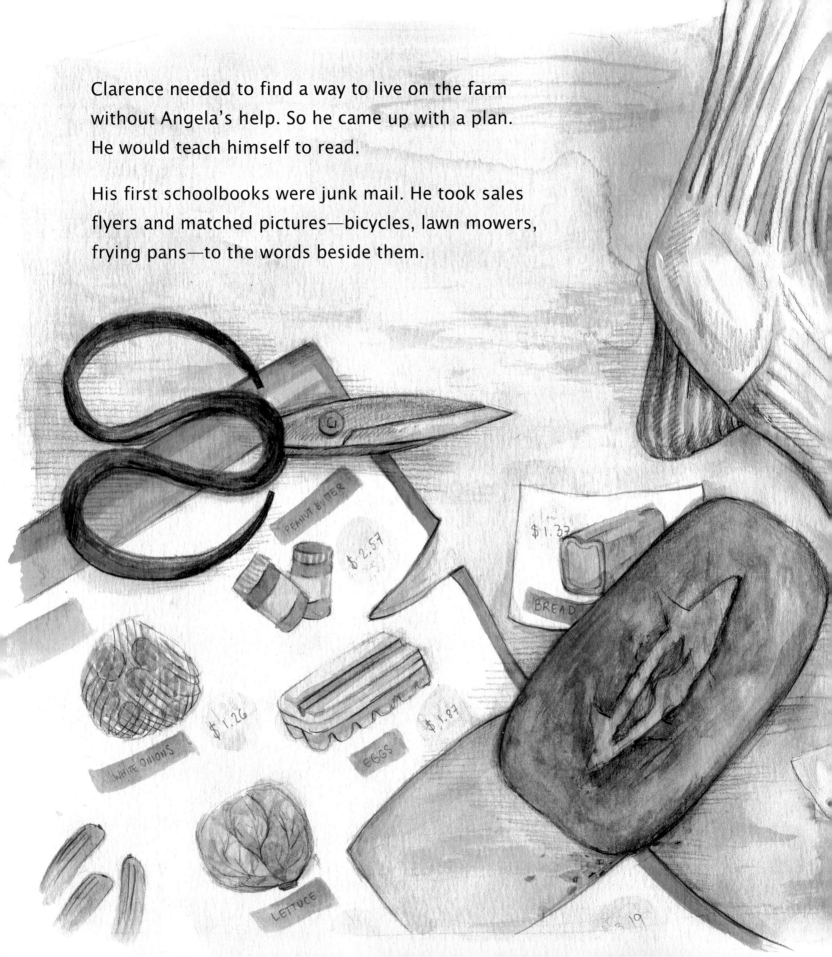

Since he couldn't make a shopping list, he cut labels off packages at home and matched them to items on the grocery store shelves.

One day, his daughter Doris found him studying a flyer and mumbling to himself. "What are you doing, Dad?" she asked.

Clarence had no choice. For just the second time in his life, he shared his secret.

Doris had been a schoolteacher. "Would you like me to teach you how to read?" she asked.

Clarence said he would. And so he became his daughter's oldest student.

"My best student ever," Doris boasted.

Clarence learned quickly. And then he read and read and read. He devoured books. He pored over newspapers. When he turned 100, he read all the cards he received.

Best of all, Clarence went back to school . . . to read to students and tell them his story. And people listened! They were amazed to hear about the man who had learned to read when he was nearly 100 years old. Once again, Clarence was the biggest person in the class. But this time, no one laughed.

A Note from the Authors

Clarence Edgar Brazier was born August 28, 1906, in a log farmhouse near Magnetawan in Ontario, Canada. He was the third of seven children. After Clarence's father was blinded in an accident, the family struggled to make ends meet. Clarence was responsible for running their farm by the time he was seven. Even if he had wanted to go back to school, his help was needed at home.

Clarence was smart, creative, hardworking, and resilient. He became a successful farmer, a good husband and father, an accomplished knitter, the head of his local farmers' union, the president of a local political party, and much more. But he never learned to read or write—at least, not until he was almost 100 years old!

How did the inability to read affect Clarence's life? People who are illiterate can't read maps, medication instructions, recipes, menus, or anything else. They cannot fill out a job application, understand some road signs, use a computer, or make a shopping list. Imagine, in a world that is filled with written words, not being able to understand any of them!

In fact, many people can't read:

- In Canada, 17 percent of adults are considered illiterate. That's more than 4.6 million adults who can't read. In the United States, 14 percent of adults— more than 32 million people—are illiterate.

- Around the world, there are more than 750 million illiterate adults. And this number is not evenly divided between genders: women make up 63 percent of illiterate adults worldwide.

- Globally, one in ten children and youth—263 million young people, more of them girls than boys—don't go to school. There are many reasons, including poverty, armed conflicts, early marriage, domestic work, and cultural beliefs.

- July 12 is Malala Day, a reminder that many girls around the world still lack the basic right to an education.

Clarence's story underlines the power of reading and how it can change a person's life—even at 100 years old! Clarence read for at least two hours every day. This habit and sharing his love of reading with students and adults brought him great joy. In 2008, at the age of 102, Clarence became the oldest person to receive the Governor General's Caring Canadian Award. He was celebrated for being "an inspirational role model for many young people ... to stay in school and to get an education." He even got a hug from Canada's governor general!

On April 15, 2012, Clarence died at the age of 105, leaving behind one of the most inspiring stories of the century.

For Fisher and Sadie,
whom I have the
privilege of reading
with every night
— C.M.C.

For Doris and Jim
Villemaire, who brought
Clarence to live with
them at Don's Pond
— R.M.

To Thérèse I.
— M.C.M.

Text © 2020 Roy MacGregor and Christine MacGregor Cation | Illustrations © 2020 Mathilde Cinq-Mars

Owlkids Books acknowledges the financial support of the Canada Council for the Arts, the Ontario Arts Council, the Government of Canada through the Canada Book Fund (CBF) and the Government of Ontario through the Ontario Creates Book Initiative for our publishing activities.

Published in Canada by Owlkids Books Inc., 1 Eglinton Avenue East, Toronto, ON M4P 3A1
Published in the US by Owlkids Books Inc., 1700 Fourth Street, Berkeley, CA 94710

Library of Congress Control Number: 2019947231

Library and Archives Canada Cataloguing in Publication

Title: Clarence's big secret / by Christine MacGregor Cation & Roy MacGregor ; Illustrated by Mathilde Cinq-Mars
Names: MacGregor Cation, Christine, author. | MacGregor, Roy, 1948- author. | Cinq-Mars, Mathilde, 1988- illustrator.
Identifiers: Canadiana 2019012458X | ISBN 9781771473316 (hardcover)
Subjects: LCSH: Brazier, Clarence, 1906-2012—Juvenile literature. | LCSH: Illiterate persons—Canada—Biography—Juvenile literature. | LCSH: Literacy—Canada—Juvenile literature.
Classification: LCC LC154 .M33 2019 | DDC j305.5/6—dc23

Edited by Debbie Rogosin | Designed by Alisa Baldwin

Photo on page 31 courtesy of Roy MacGregor. Background photo on page 30/31 © Vladimir A/Dreamstime

Manufactured in Shenzhen, Guangdong, China, in October 2019, by WKT Co. Ltd.
Job #19CB1110

A   B   C   D   E   F

Publisher of Chirp, Chickadee and OWL
www.owlkidsbooks.com | Owlkids Books is a division of